First published in the United States, Great Britain, Canada, Australia, and New Zealand in 2008 by North-South Books Inc., an imprint of NordSüd Verlag AG, Zürich, Switzerland.
Distributed in the United States by North-South Books Inc., New York.

Library of Congress Cataloging-in-Publication Data is available.
ISBN: 978-0-7358-2207-8 (trade edition).
10 9 8 7 6 5 4 3 2 1

Printed in Belgium

www.northsouth.com

Anna's Wish

by **Bruno Hächler** • *illustrated by* **Friederike Rave**

NorthSouth
New York / London

It had not snowed for many years. Summer turned to fall, and the leaves fell from the trees. Fall turned to winter, and fog fell over the city like a gray blanket. But no snow.

At first people thought nothing of it. Each winter, grown-ups got out their snow shovels. Children drew pictures of snowmen and sleds. Surely snow would fall soon.

But when the first crocuses popped out of the ground, people put their shovels away and turned their thoughts to spring.

Winter followed winter without a flake of snow. Bundled up in their coats, people looked sadly at the sky. Many began to forget how once the snow had sparkled on their city, covering it like a thick, white blanket.

Then, one day, Anna and her mother were walking past the bakery. Suddenly Anna felt something very soft and cold touch her cheek, as light as a butterfly's kiss. Just as suddenly, it was gone.

A week later, as they passed the bakery, Anna felt it again—the tiniest cold touch. Was someone playing a trick on her?

Anna stopped and looked around. Staring back at her through the bakery window was a little white horse, standing on a cake. His coat sparkled with sugar crystals . . . or was it ice? He stood on a pile of white frosting that looked like . . .

"What's snow like?" Anna asked her mother.

"Hmmm." Her mother sighed. "The last time I saw snow, I was just a little girl like you." She smiled. "It was wonderful—white and cold and sparkling."

"Tell me more!" begged Anna.

"We played in the snow for hours and hours," her mother said. "We made snowmen with round bellies and carrot noses. We went sledding.

"We caught snowflakes on our tongues, and they fell on our coats like stars. Each one is different, you know—not a single snowflake is exactly like another."

"If only it would snow again!" said Anna.

That evening, in a dusty corner of the basement, Anna found an old wooden sled. It was dirty and the paint was peeling, but Anna didn't care. She carried it up the basement stairs.

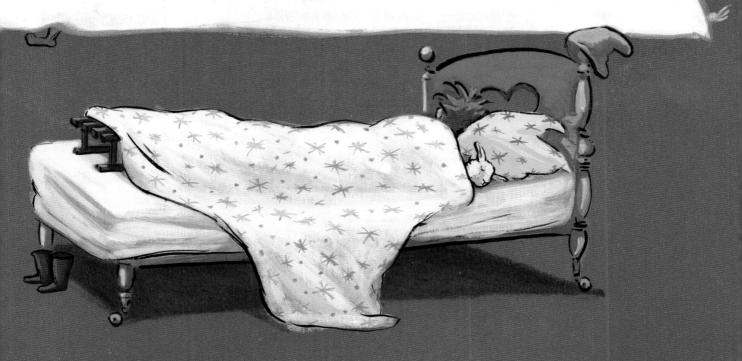

In her room, Anna wiped the dust from the sled. Then she tried it out. She imagined dashing down a snowy hill, the wind whistling in her ears, the snow spraying her face. That night, she dreamed of snow.

The next morning, Anna was out of bed early.
After breakfast, she hurried to the bakery. There was
the little white horse. He seemed to be expecting her.
Anna put her hands on the window. Her nose almost
touched the glass. Did the little horse move closer too?

"Oh, little snow horse," thought Anna, "I wish . . .
I wish . . . I wish . . . I wish . . ."

Harder than she had ever wished for anything,
Anna wished for snow.

Like tiny stars, her wishes floated up into the sky and froze. Then, slowly, they began to fall back down to the earth.

They fell gently, swinging and swaying, more and more and more of them. Hundreds of them. Thousands of them. Millions of them. They fell on the city, covering the streets and the houses, the bushes and the trees.

People came running out of their houses,
laughing and dancing. "It's snowing!" they called
to one another. Soon snow shovels were scraping
porches and sidewalks. Children threw snowballs
and began building snowmen.

"Thank you," whispered Anna.
The little horse might have winked his eye, but so much snow was coming down that Anna couldn't be sure. She lifted her face and felt the cold flakes touch her cheeks, as soft as butterfly kisses.

Then she pulled her hat down over her ears
and ran out into the snow.